The GRAPE JELLY MYSTERY

Written by Olive Blake

Illustrated by Joan E. Goodman

Troll Associates

Troll Associates, Mahwah, N.J.

Library of Congress Catalog Card Number: 78-18040

"Grape jelly!" said Sparky.

"Peanut butter!" said Nell.

"Sliced banana!" said Arthur. "And marshmallow fluff!"

"Delicious!" said Sparky.

"Delightful!" said Nell.

"Hurry!" cried Arthur. "I'm starving to death!"

Sparky opened the jelly jar. He spread grape jelly on a slice of white bread.

Nell stuck her finger into the peanut butter. "Mmmmmm," she said. "It's chunky!" She put lots of peanut butter on a second slice of bread.

"Ta *da*!" sang Arthur. "Here comes the best part." He covered a third piece of bread with banana slices and marshmallow fluff.

"Yummy, yummy, in my tummy," he sang. He covered the sandwich with a fourth slice of bread, and took a giant bite.

Nell took a bite.

Sparky took a bite.

Arthur took two bites.

"Hey!" said Sparky. "Leave some for us!"

"Be careful," said Nell. "It's dripping. It's getting all over everything."

Sparky got a sponge. He wiped marshmallow fluff off the table. He wiped it off the chair. He wiped it off the geranium.

He wiped peanut butter off his spelling book. He wiped it off the sugar bowl. He wiped it off the cat.

He wiped grape jelly off the bird cage. He wiped it off his sleeve. He wiped it off a piece of paper.

"Hey!" said Sparky. "Look at this! It's a note from Mom." He showed the paper to Nell.

"Read it," said Arthur. "What does it say?"

"Some of the letters are smeared," said Nell.

"Let me read it," said Sparky. "I am the oldest." He took the note from Nell. *Important!* (he read) *I went to the* (something) *store* ...

"What is a *something* store?" asked Arthur.

"I can't read that word," said Sparky. "The first two letters are gloppy from grape jelly."

"Let's copy the note on another piece of paper," said Nell. "Then we can figure it out together."

"We can decode it," said Sparky.

"Like real detectives," said Arthur.

Nell got a pencil and a piece of paper.
Then, she wrote:

Important! I went to the _ _ t store. Be
sure everything is ready. See you soon. Love
and kisses, Mom.

"Ready for what?" asked Sparky.

"Beats me," said Arthur.

"If we only knew where Mom went," said Nell.

"She went to a store," said Sparky.

"But what kind of a store?" asked Nell.

"A store that has three letters and ends with a *t*," said Arthur.

"I have a good idea," said Nell. "Let's all think of three-letter stores."

"Great!" said Sparky.

"Super brilliant!" said Arthur.

"It was nothing," said Nell.

They thought and they thought and they thought. "I know," said Arthur. "It's an *ant* store! Mom went to an ant store to buy me some ants. She knows how much I want an ant farm."

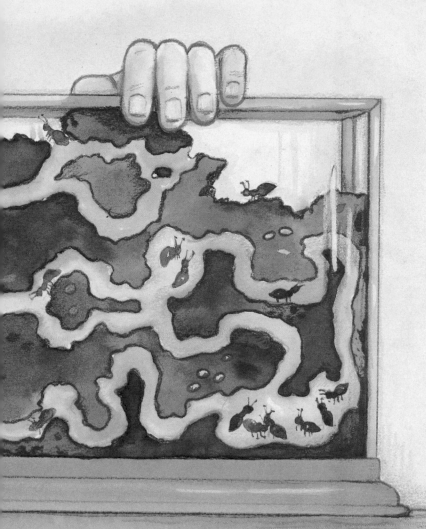

"She says to have everything ready,"
said Sparky. "What does she mean by that?"
"She means I have to clean my room,"
said Arthur. "Mom always says *Don't even
talk to me until your room is clean!*"

Arthur looked at his room. "I don't
know if it's worth it," he said.

He thought about the ant farm. Then he
made his bed. He picked up three soggy
towels, and threw them into the hamper. He
put away his sneakers and his slippers and

his boots. He folded his pajamas and a green
sweatshirt that said SMILE. He picked up
his crayons. He kicked his skates under the
bed. He put his cowboy hat on his dresser
and said, "There! This room is clean enough
for the fussiest ant!"

When he went downstairs, Nell said:

"I don't think Mom went to an ant store.
I think she went to an *art* store. She knows
how much I need some new paintbrushes.
I'm sure that's where she went. She went to
an art store."

"Get a broom!" said Arthur.

Nell made her bed. She picked up her rock collection. She dusted her shell collection. She arranged her broken glass collection. She hid her bottle cap collection. Then she threw out a dried-up orange peel, and hung up a poster that said HAVE A NICE DAY!

When she was all finished, Sparky said:

"I don't think Mom went to an art store. I think she went to a *bat* store. She knows my good bat is broken. That's where she went. She went to a bat store."

"Oh, no!" cried Nell. "I cleaned my room for nothing!"

Sparky made his bed. He picked up two chewing gum wrappers and one popsicle stick. He put his turtle back in its bowl, and his comic books back on the shelf. He hung up his blue jeans and his red sweater and a banner that said IT'S NICE TO BE IMPOR-TANT. BUT IT'S MORE IMPORTANT TO BE NICE.

When Sparky's room was clean, Arthur said:

"Maybe it's a *cat* store, or a *cot* store, or a *cut* store. How can you be sure?"

"We have two cots," said Sparky. "We don't need a third one."

"We have a cat," said Nell.

"What about a cut store?" asked Arthur.
"I get lots of cuts. Maybe Mom is buying
bandages, and stuff like that."

"Take a nap," said Sparky.

"Have a banana," said Nell.

"Maybe it's an *eat* store," said Arthur. "I bet Mom is bringing a surprise for supper."

"Pizza!" said Sparky.

"Fried chicken!" said Nell.

"And we are supposed to set the table," said Arthur.

"That's it," said Nell.

"Oh, boy!" said Sparky. "Pizza!"

Arthur got the napkins and the glasses.
Nell got the plates. Sparky got the knives
and forks and spoons.

"Let's surprise Mom," said Nell.
"Let's make the kitchen extra nice."

So Arthur swept the floor. Sparky cut some flowers and put them on the table. Nell made place cards for everybody. She drew a picture on each one.

When they were finished, Arthur said:

"Suppose it's a *fat* store."

"Suppose you stop supposing," said Sparky.

"It could be a *hat* store," said Nell. "Maybe Mom is buying a new hat. That's where she went. She went to a hat store to buy a hat for herself!"

"Then what are we supposed to get ready?" asked Arthur.

"Maybe Mom wants us to clean *her* room," said Nell.

"That's not fair," said Sparky. "If Mom is getting a new hat, she should clean her *own* room."

"Mom never wears a hat," said Arthur. "She wears earmuffs."

"That's true," said Nell. "Where could she be?"

"Maybe she went to a *mat* store," said Sparky. "I heard her say our old doormat is falling apart."

"Dad said we were getting a new one," said Arthur.

"That must be it," said Nell. "I suppose Mom wants us to clean the front porch."

"I'm getting tired of supposing," said Arthur.

"I'll sweep," said Sparky.

"I'll put the bicycles away," said Nell.

"I'll rest," said Arthur.

"Arthur!" said Nell.

"I'll shake out the smelly old doormat," said Arthur.

When they were finished, they sat down
on the steps.

"We did everything," said Sparky. "We cleaned our rooms. We set the table. We swept the kitchen. We cleaned the front porch. We are ready for anything."

"Maybe Mom went to a *nut* store," said
Arthur.

"Not a chance," said Sparky. "We
already have a nut. Only one nut to a
family."

"It could be a *pit* store, or a *pot* store,
or . . ."

Just then, a blue station wagon drove up to the house.

"It's Mom!" they shouted. They jumped up and ran to meet her.

"Where were you?" asked Nell.

"What did you get?" asked Sparky.

"Did you bring a surprise for me?" asked Arthur.

"Sillies," said their mother. "Today is Tuesday. Don't tell me you forgot about Tuesday."

"It's Tuesday!" cried Nell.

"The *pet* store!" cried Arthur.

"Our puppy!" cried Sparky. "How did we ever forget?"

They ran to the car. On the front seat
was a small brown puppy. It had a white
spot on its head. It had another white spot
on the tip of its tail.

Arthur carried the puppy in his arms.
"It's Tuesday," he sang as he hurried up the
steps.

At the front door, the children's mother said:

"Whatever happened to our dusty old porch?"

In the kitchen, their mother said:
"How beautiful the table looks! Flowers!
Place cards! What a lovely surprise!"
"Wait till you see our rooms," said
Arthur. "You are going to faint!"

"Everything is ready," said Sparky. "We didn't forget a thing."

"Did you remember to make a bed for the new puppy?" his mother asked.

"Rats!" said Arthur. "We forgot!"

"No matter," said their mother. "We will make the bed together. We will make a soft and cozy bed for our new little puppy. But right now, I'm starved." Then she paused.

"Would someone please fix me a grape jelly sandwich?"